Life Through The Eyes Of A Butterfly

by: Sean A. Wilson

Hunter Heart Publishing
DuPont, Washington

To order products, or for any other correspondence:

Hunter Heart Publishing
P.O. Box 354
DuPont, Washington 98327
Tel. (253) 906-2160 – Fax: (253) 912-1667
E-mail: publisher@hunterheartpublishing.com
Or reach us on the internet: www.hunterheartpublishing.com

"Offering God's Heart to a Dying World"

This book and all other Hunter Heart Publishing™ books are available at Christian bookstores and distributors worldwide.

Chief Editor: Brenda Mates

Illustrator: Brian Bear
Cover format and logos: Exousia Marketing Group www.exousiamg.com

ISBN: 978-1-937741-92-1

Printed by:

BookMasters, Inc.
30 Amberwood Pkwy.
Ashland, Ohio 44805
Printed January, 2012
Job Number: D8849

For Worldwide Distribution, Printed in the United States of America.

Dedication

"This Book is dedicated to my Family: Janice, Sean II, and Anihya as a beacon of inspiration to all children. I believe all children who read, or are read this book, will be inspired to seek God first and accomplish all that He has predestined for them to do."

I prayed that God would change me.

I woke up from my sleep
in a thick silk sheet

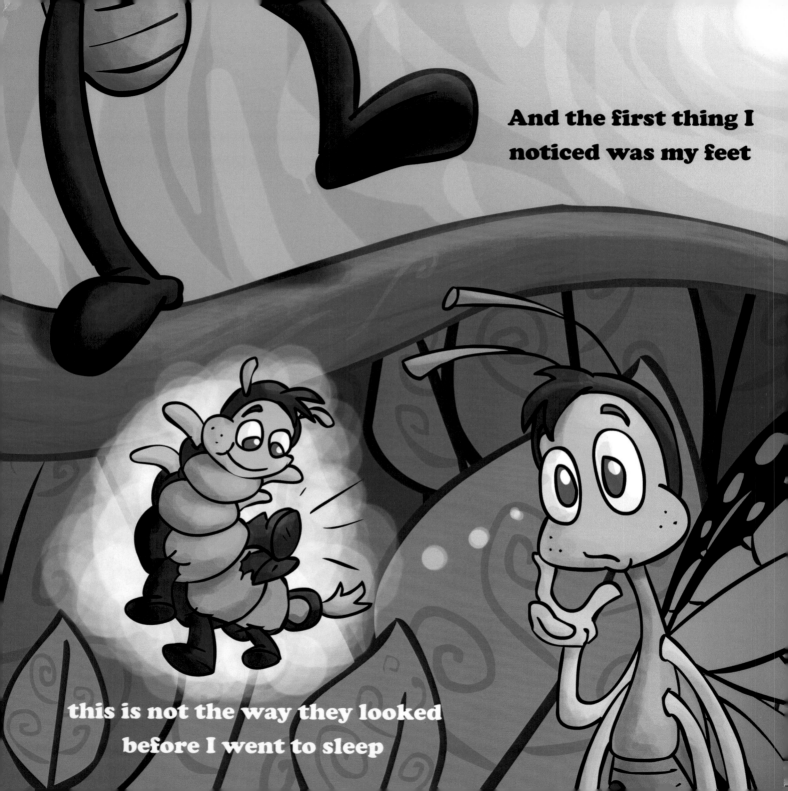

Man, it really looks like part of me is still inside.

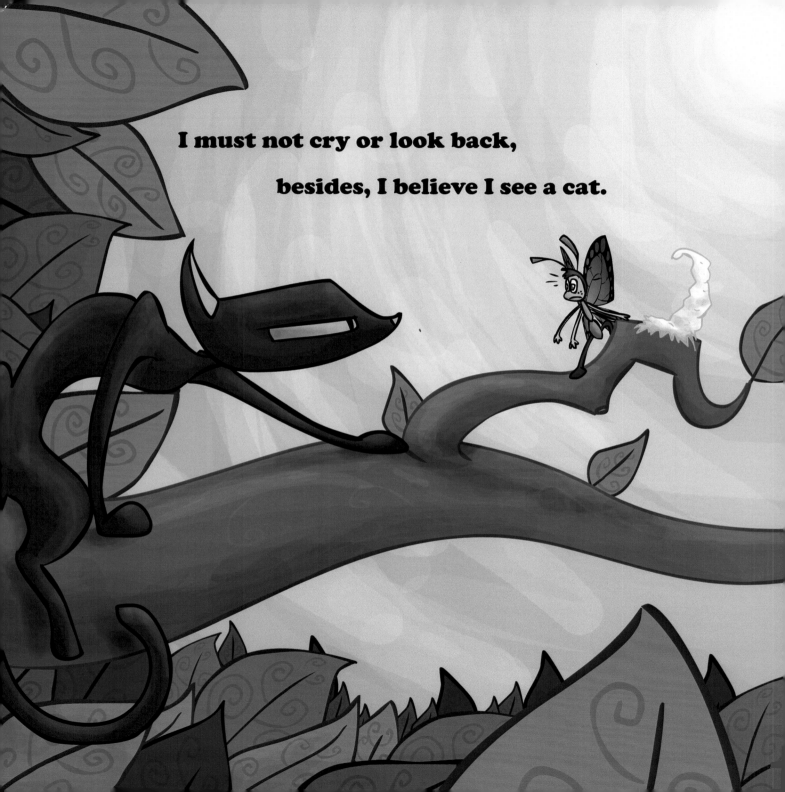

I must not cry or look back,

besides, I believe I see a cat.

Who cares,
at least I'm safe.

The winds are strong
and blowing me around;

it's time to take a rest on the ground.

That was fun, I felt so free;

God has surely been
a blessing to me.

God changed my life in a blink of an eye

and from this point on I will always fly.

The End.